Contents

Crayon Spinosaurus

Pencil crayons are ideal for drawing and colouring. Build up richness by layering colours, or create exciting textures by scribbling.

You will need:
- Pencil crayons
- Drawing paper

1 Use a dark blue crayon to draw an oval for the Spinosaurus's body.

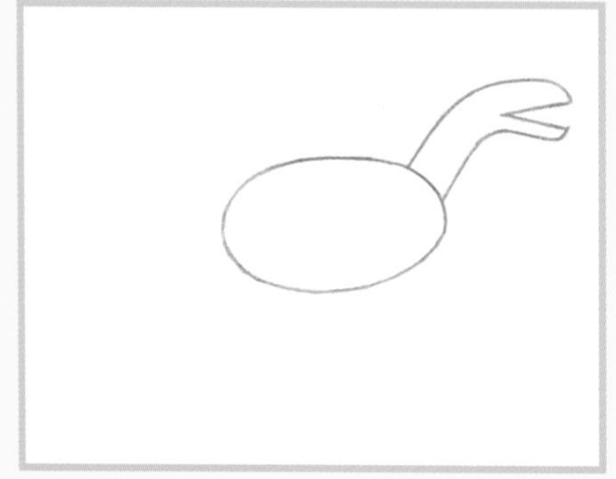

2 Now draw in its neck, head and mouth.

3 Draw in the Spinosaurus's back legs.

4 Draw in the Spinosaurus's short arms and three-fingered hands. Add its long tail.

5 Draw the shape of the Spinosaurus's sail and add lines for the spines.

6 Draw in an eye, nostril and teeth. Add its clawed feet and a line for its belly. Now add spots!

Use light blue pencil crayon to colour in the Spinosaurus's head, neck, body, tail, legs and arms.

Colour in its sail, belly and eye with pale yellow pencil crayon. Colour in the spots with orange crayon and its claws with dark blue.

Draw in some trees, and a tree fern. Add a lake and a grey cloudy sky. Now colour in the background.

Waxy Diplodocus

Draw onto paper with a wax crayon and paint over it with watercolour paints. The water-based paint will run off the wax line drawing.

You will need:
- Wax crayons
- Thick cartridge paper
- Watercolour paints
- Paintbrush

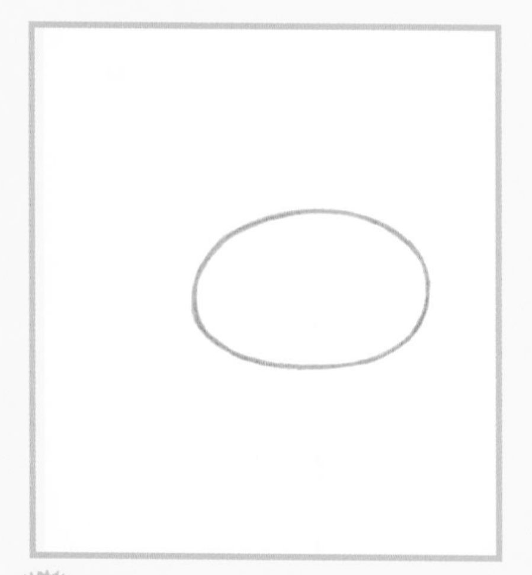

1 Draw the Diplodocus's body with a wax crayon.

2 Then draw the shape of its long neck and head.

3 Add four sturdy legs.

4 Draw a long, curving tail. Add the top of its head, an eye, nose and mouth.

5 Add a zigzag pattern down its back and tail.

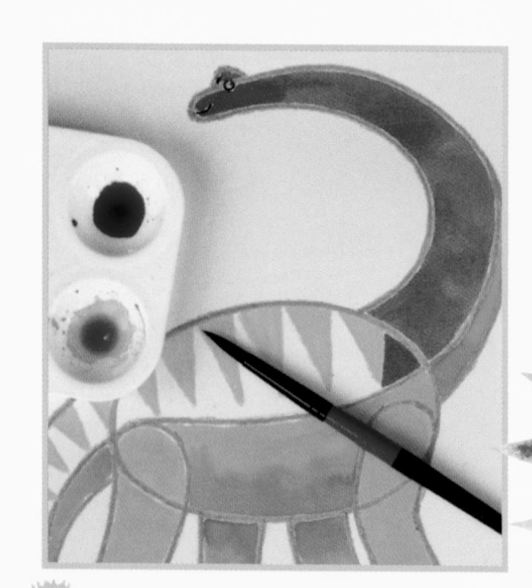

6 Paint the Diplodocus with red, yellow and orange watercolour paints.

Draw a tree fern and some shrubs for the Diplodocus to eat. Add some hills in the background, then paint over it with watercolours.

Tissue paper T. rex

Draw a Tyrannosaurus rex with a felt-tip pen. Then glue lots of scraps of tissue paper over it to add colour and texture.

You will need:

- Black felt-tip pen
- Thick cartridge paper
- Coloured tissue paper
- PVA glue

1 Use a felt-tip pen to draw the dinosaur's body.

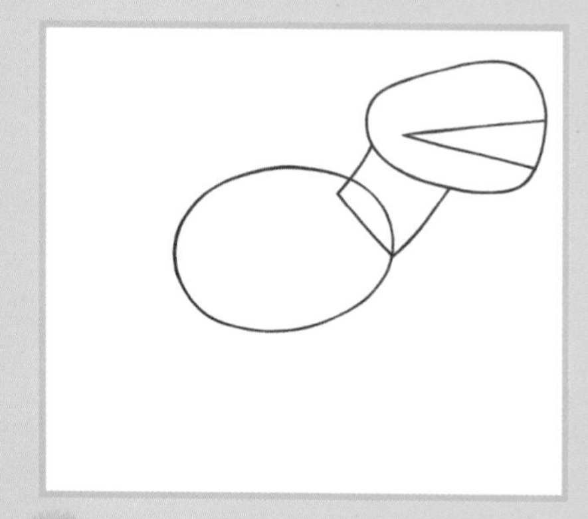

2 Add simple shapes for its neck and head.

3 Add two sturdy legs and small front arms.

4 Draw in both feet and an extra claw on its back leg. Add a long tail.

5 Draw in the eye ridge, eyes, nostril and teeth. Add a line for its underbelly.

6 Tear yellow, green and blue tissue paper into small pieces and glue onto your dinosaur's body.

Tear out blue and purple tissue paper spots to glue onto the Tyrannosaurus's front leg, its back and tail (as shown).

Glue on tissue paper to make a volcano in the background.

Finish off its eyes and nostrils by gluing on pieces of torn black tissue paper.

Tear thin pieces of tissue paper for the ferns, and glue in place.

Chalk Velociraptor

Chalks can be used in many different ways. Try scribbling with the tip, or lay the chalk on its side to make a broad band of colour. Use your fingertip to smudge the chalk to create a soft effect.

You will need:

- Black paper
- White chalk
- Coloured chalks
- Scrap paper to rest your drawing hand on

1 Use pale brown chalk to draw the dinosaur's head.

2 Now add simple shapes for its neck and body.

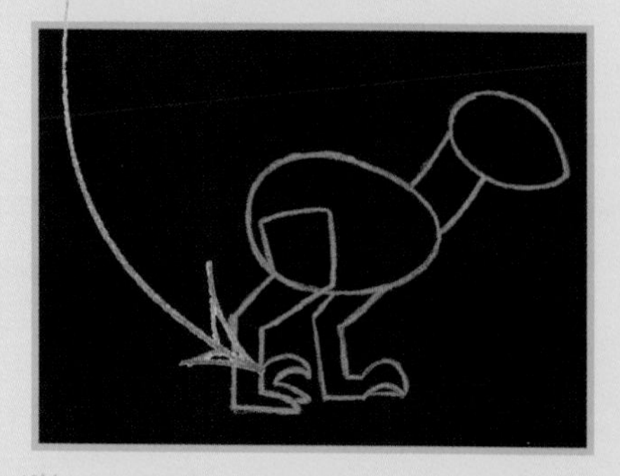

3 Draw in its legs, feet and toes. Add a big curved toe claw to each foot.

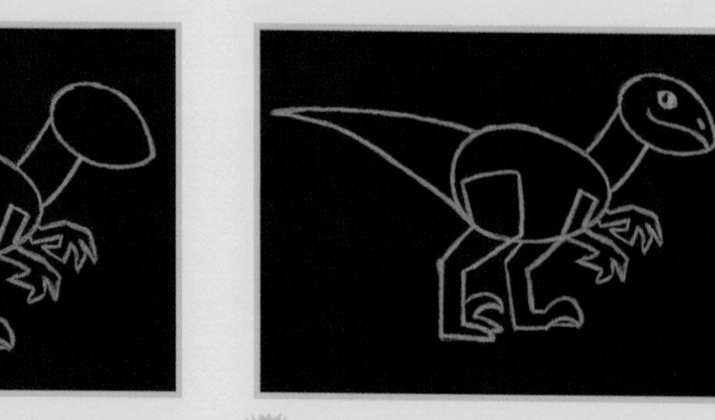

4 Add Velociraptor's arms and three-fingered hands.

5 Draw in the tail. Add its mouth and nostril. Use green and yellow chalk to draw its eye.

6 Now draw its teeth. Add feathery hairs to its head and arms.

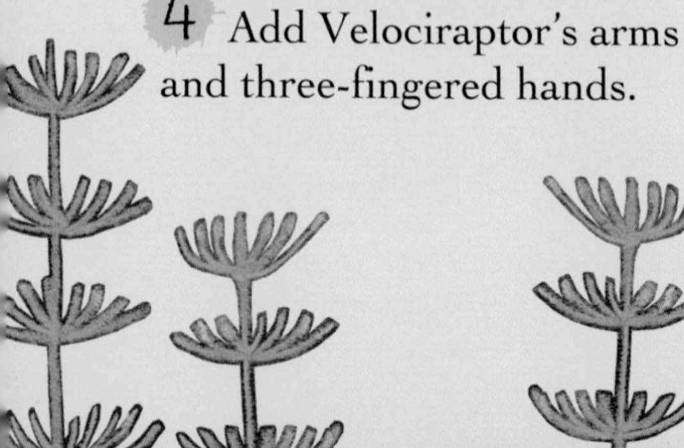

7 Use pale brown and yellow chalks to draw feather-like hair on the Velociraptor's head, neck, body, legs and tail. Gently smudge the lines with your fingertip.

Draw in the background and smudge areas to soften the effect.

Painted Shapes Parasaurolophus

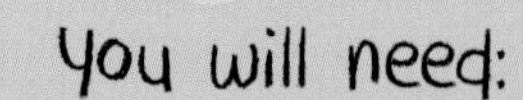
You will need:

- Poster paints
- Paintbrush
- Cartridge paper
- Black felt-tip pen

Build up the shape of a Parasaurolophus by painting a series of simple shapes. Then draw in the final details using a felt-tip pen.

1 Paint an oval shape for the Parasaurolophus's body.

2 Paint a triangle for its head, then add a sausage shape for its neck.

3 Paint in two long rectangles for the back legs.

4 Paint in two thin shapes for the Parasaurolophus's front legs.

5 Paint in a large triangle for its tail, and a long curved shape for its head crest. Add toenails.

6 Use a black felt-tip pen to draw its eye, nostril and mouth. Add black stripes to its neck and body.

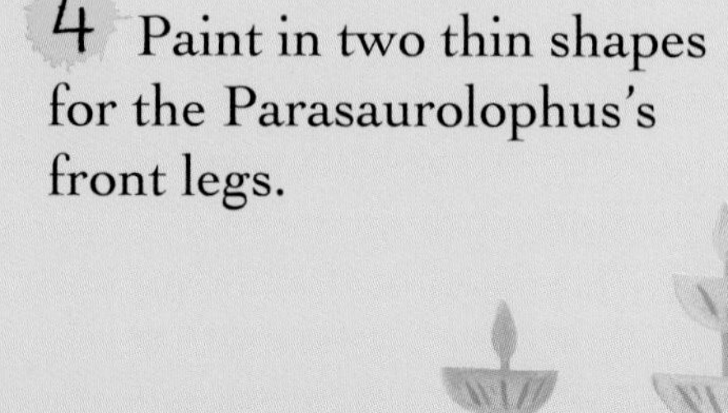

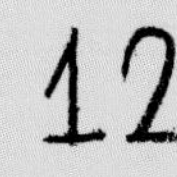

Paint in a steep hill and some trees. Add mountains in the background and a pale yellow sky with a large orange sun.

Paint grey stripes on the Parasaurolophus's crest. Add some pine needles for it to munch for lunch!

Use the black felt-tip pen to draw in its knees and to outline its toenails.

Paint in a waterhole to drink at, and some horsetails growing nearby.

Handprint Triceratops

You will need:
- Poster paints
- Large paintbrush
- Small paintbrush
- Coloured paper
- Felt-tip pen
- Scissors
- PVA glue

Have fun making your own painted handprint and then turn it into a scary Triceratops!

1 Paint your hand with poster paint and press it firmly onto the paper. Leave your print to dry.

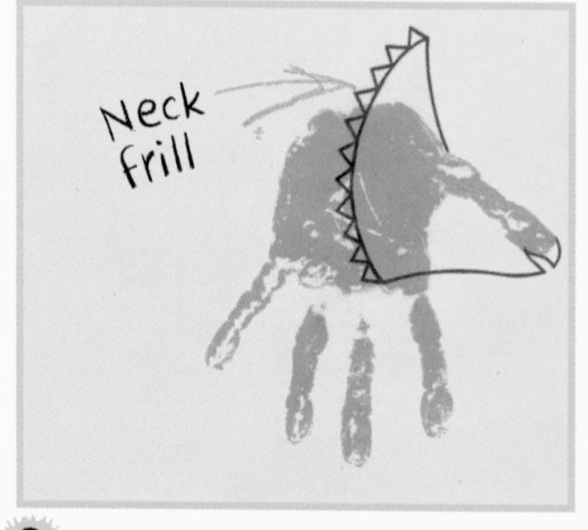

2 Use a black felt-tip pen to draw in the Triceratops' neck frill and mouth.

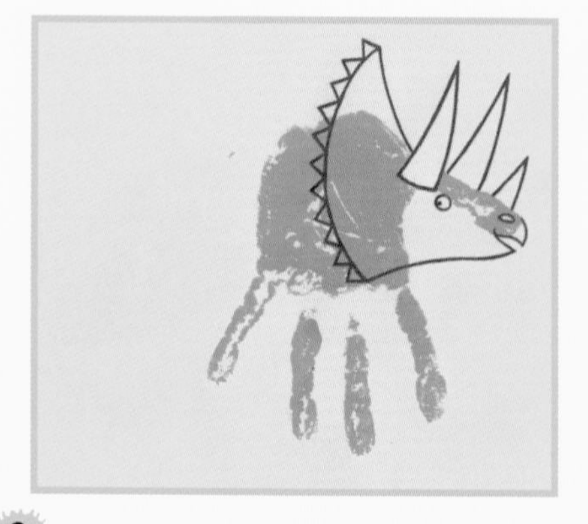

3 Now draw in its three large horns. Add an eye and a nostril.

4 Draw in Triceratops' big tail and its toenails.

5 Use the poster paints to paint in the Triceratops' eye and horns. Add stripes to its tail.

6 Cut around the Triceratops. Glue it onto a sheet of coloured paper.

Using the poster paints, make some 'fingerprint plants' for your Triceratops to eat.

Here are some more dinosaur handprint ideas for you to draw and paint.

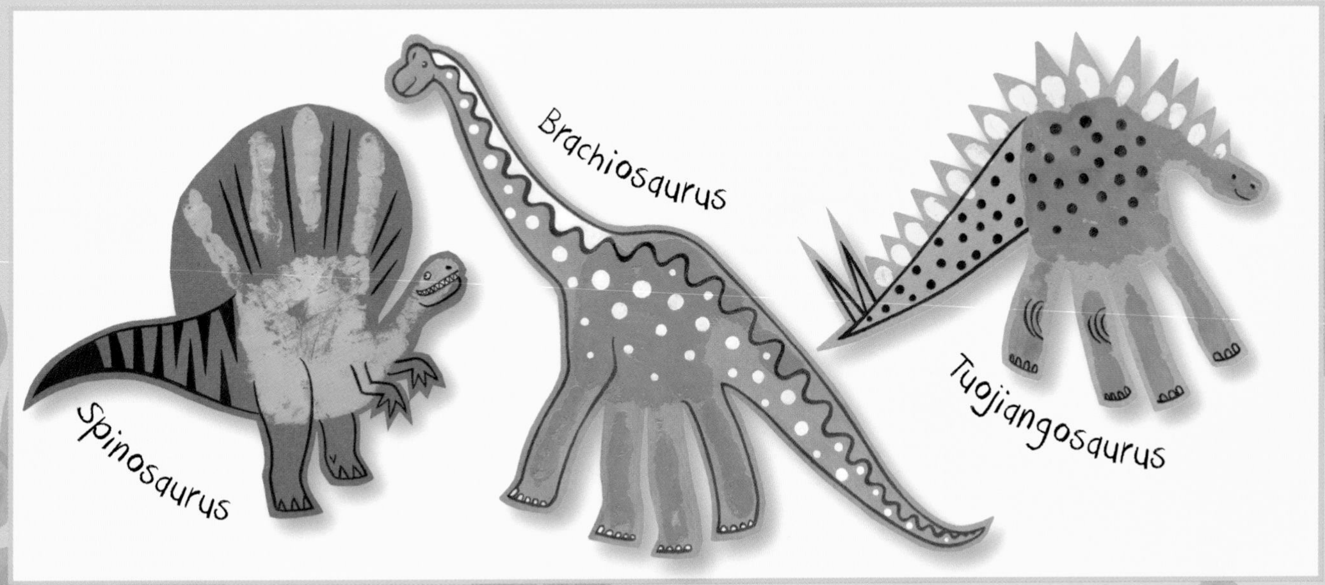

Paper Cup Dinosaurs

Invent an awesome dinosaur and use it to create a paper cup monster.

You will need:

- Paper cups
- Poster paints
- Paintbrushes
- PVA glue
- Scissors
- Pencil
- Thick paper

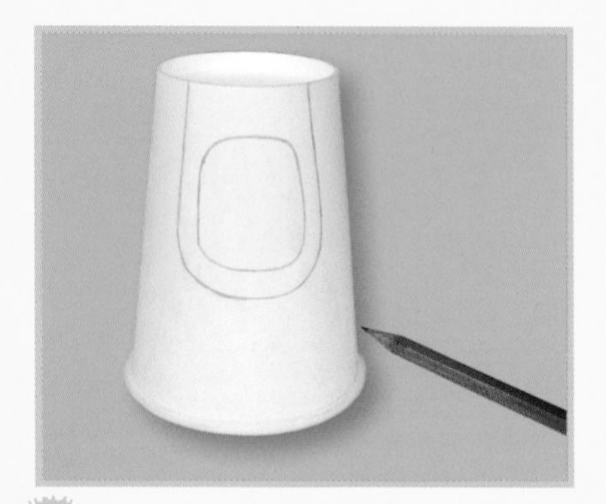

1 Draw in the shape of your dinosaur's head with its mouth wide open.

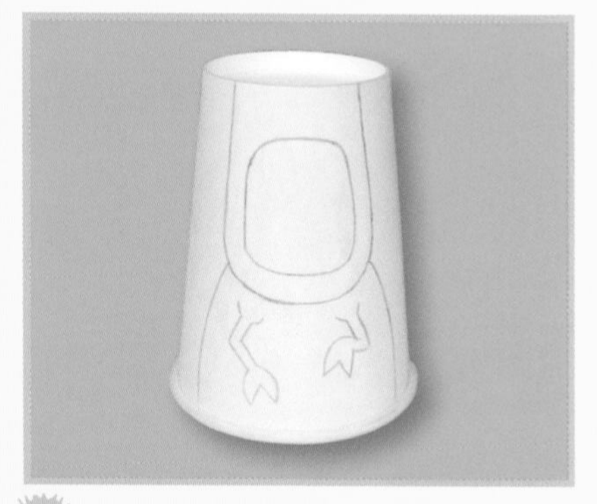

2 Draw a curved shape for the dinosaur's chest. Add two small arms.

3 Now draw in its pointed teeth and big long tongue.

4 Add the nostrils. Draw a curved line for its back with added zigzags (as shown).

5 Paint your dinosaur brown and blue. Make its tongue and nostrils red, its teeth white and the background dark green.

6 Use paper to draw and paint a tail and two eyes (as shown). When dry, cut the shapes out.

Finish off by painting a pattern of blue triangles down your dinosaur's back and tail. Add some blue dots to its chest.

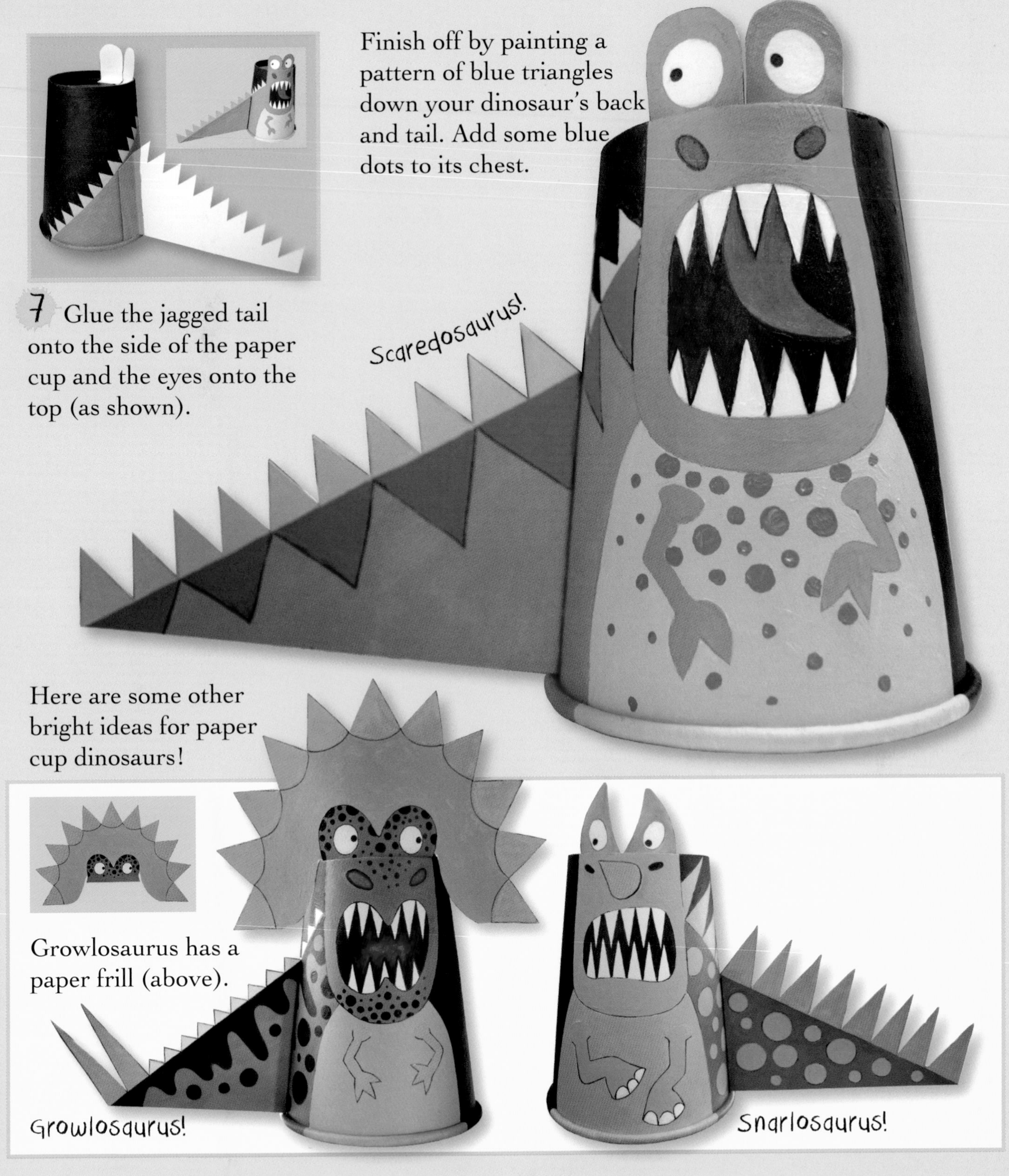

7 Glue the jagged tail onto the side of the paper cup and the eyes onto the top (as shown).

Here are some other bright ideas for paper cup dinosaurs!

Growlosaurus has a paper frill (above).

Painted Pebble Dinosaur Eggs

You will need:

- Pencil
- Poster paints
- Paintbrushes
- Large pebbles
- Fine black felt-tip pen
- Coloured paper
- Card
- PVA glue

When collecting pebbles, look for flat, smooth ones, as these will be the easiest to paint.

1 Cover the pebble with white poster paint and leave to dry.

2 Use a pencil to draw a zigzag hole in the dinosaur's eggshell.

3 Draw a rectangle for the baby dinosaur's head shape.

4 Draw in its neck and a round shape for its body.

5 Pencil in the dinosaur's eyes, nostrils and mouth. Draw in two short arms, and hands with two fingers.

6 Paint the eggshell with cream-coloured poster paint. Paint the inside of the shell black.

Paint the baby dinosaur with pink poster paint. Make its eye sockets and arms red and its hands pale pink. Add white to its teeth and eye.

Use a fine black felt-tip pen to outline the dinosaur, its eye, nostrils, mouth and teeth.

Tear thin strips of coloured paper to arrange into the shape of a dinosaur's nest. Glue these onto a large sheet of card and place your dinosaur eggs on top.

Use a black felt-tip pen to draw cracks on the eggshell. Paint some pale yellow spots on the baby dinosaur.

Painted Paper Apatosaurus

You will need:
- A4 sheet of thick paper
- Pencil
- Scissors
- Poster paints
- Paintbrush
- PVA glue

Why not make a whole herd of dinosaurs using this simple technique?

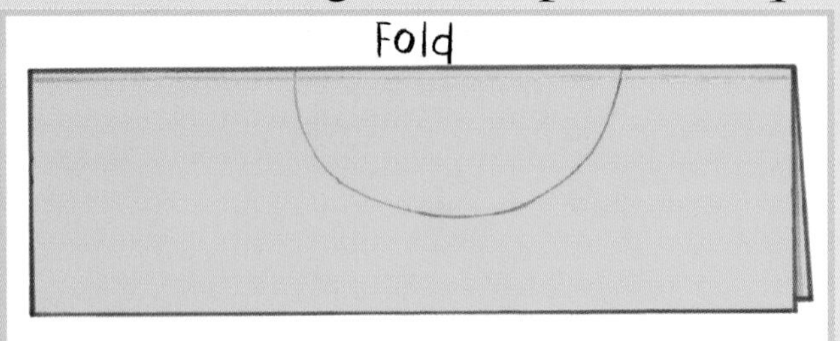

1 Paint the sheet of paper green and leave to dry. Fold it in half and draw in the shape of the Apatosaurus's body.

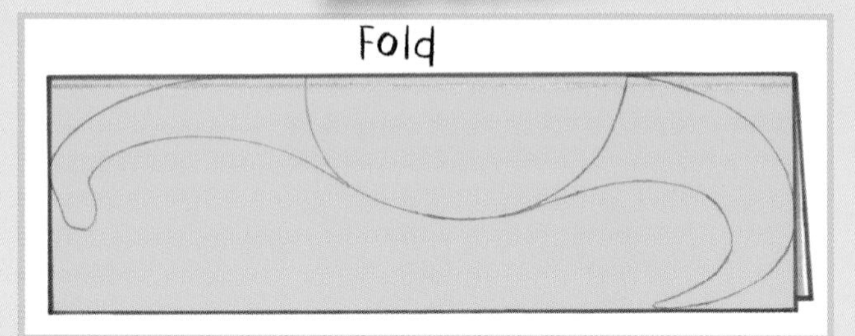

2 Now draw in the Apatosaurus's neck, head and tail.

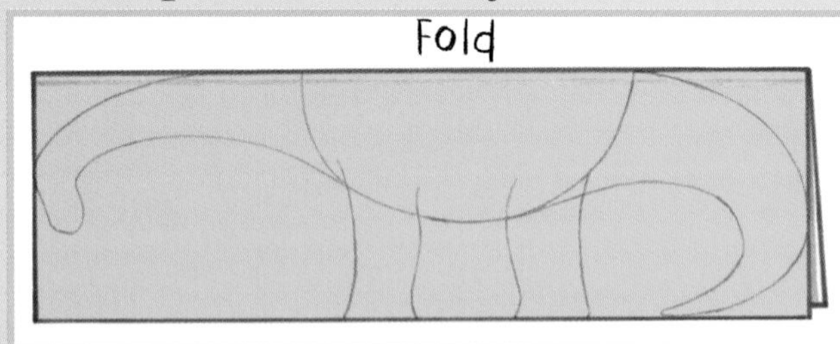

3 Then draw in the Apatosaurus's legs.

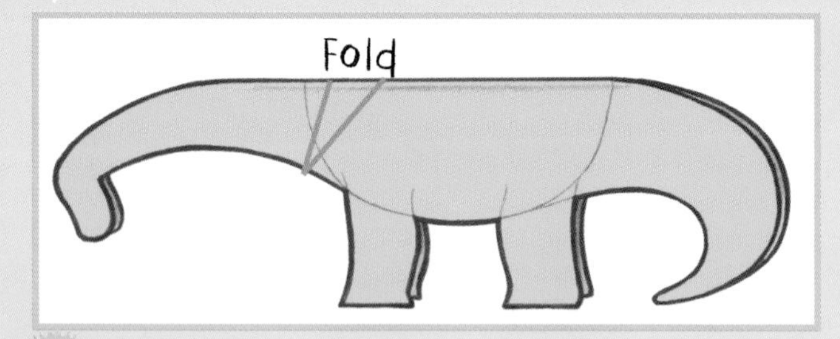

4 Cut out the dinosaur. Pencil in two angled lines on its neck (as shown).

5 Fold and crease the first pencil line (as shown). Then unfold it.

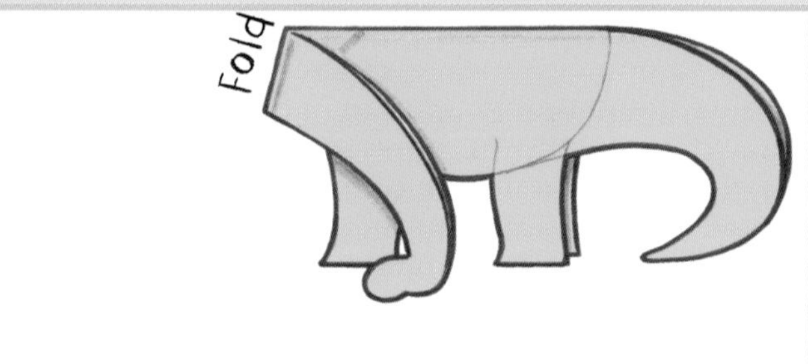

6 Now fold and crease the second pencil line. Unfold it.

7 Carefully push both foldlines behind the body (as shown). You may want to ask an adult to help.

Glue both sides of the neck and head together. Do the same with its tail.

Draw a long squiggly line down your dinosaur's neck, body and tail. Then draw big spots on the top section and paint around them using dark blue paint (as shown).

Draw and paint the dinosaur's eye, nostril, mouth and teeth.

Add toenails. Paint small yellow dots along the dinosaur's neck, belly, legs and tail.

Below are two more dinosaur ideas for you to try.

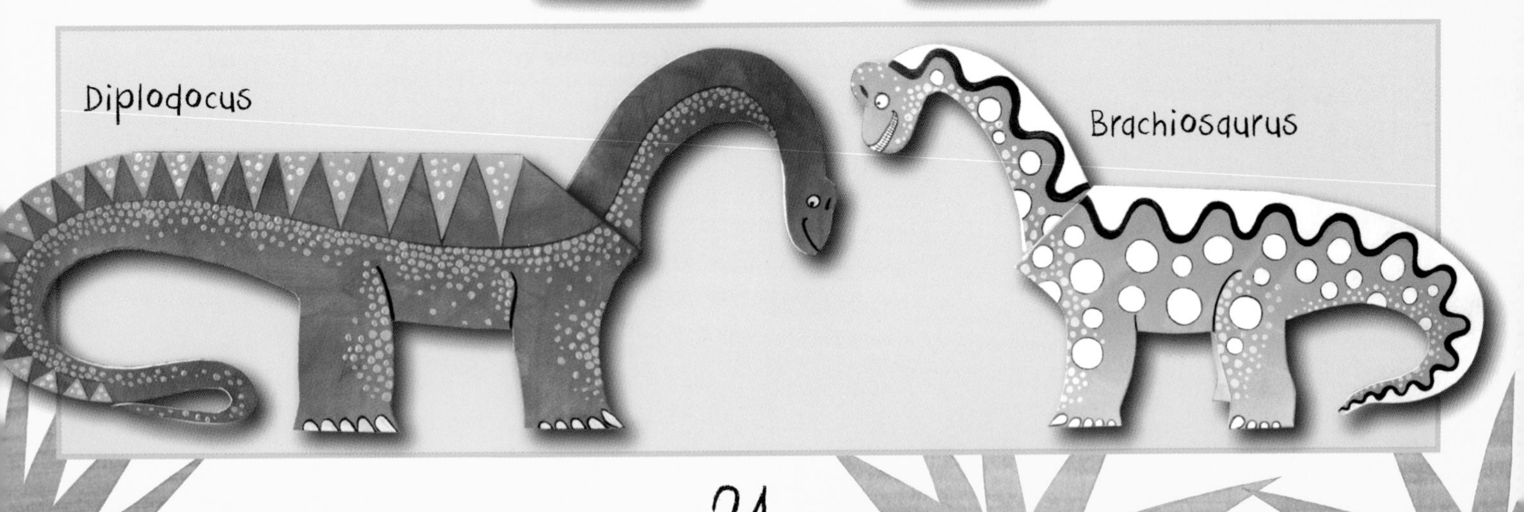

Printed Ankylosaurus

Potatoes and carrots make ideal printing blocks. Ask an adult to cut them in half or into shapes (as used here).

You will need:

- Pencil
- Felt-tip pens
- Large paintbrush
- Potatoes and carrots
- Poster paints
- Coloured paper
- Old dishwashing sponges
- Scissors
- PVA glue

1 Halve a large potato and draw around it for the shape of the Ankylosaurus's body. Use half a small potato for its head.

2 Draw around half a carrot for the tail. Use a short carrot stick for its neck, and a round slice for its tail club.

3 Draw around a thick carrot stick for each Ankylosaurus leg.

4 Paint the cut side of the potatoes red and press down firmly to print the head and body. Print the neck and tail with carrot shapes.

5 Use the thick carrot stick to print the legs, and the slice of carrot to print the tail club.

6 Cut the carrot slice in half, then half again. Use to print the spines and the bony nodules running down its back.

7 Finish by printing three spines on your Ankylosaurus's head. Use a felt-tip pen to draw in its eyes, nostrils and mouth. Then add black paint to finish.

Paint orange spots on the Ankylosaurus's neck, belly and tail. Draw and paint in its toenails.

Cut out your finished dinosaur and glue it onto a sheet of coloured paper.

Use scissors to cut the shape of a fern out of a dishwashing sponge. Cover it with paint and then print the ferns.

Painted Paper Pteranodon

You will need:

- A4 sheet of thick paper or thin card
- Poster paint
- Paintbrushes
- Pencil
- Scissors

These fantastic flying dinosaurs make great decorations.

1 Paint the sheet of paper golden yellow. Leave to dry.

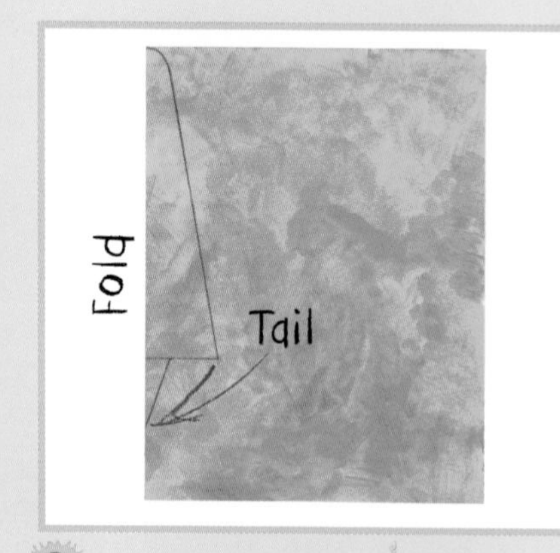

2 Fold the paper in half. Pencil in a triangle for the Pteranodon's head and body. Add its tail.

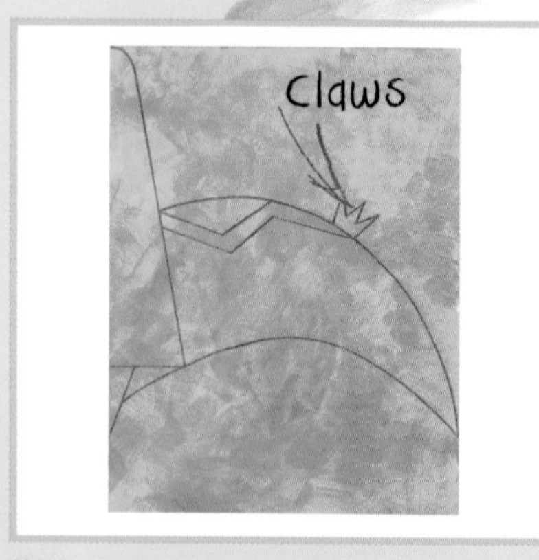

3 Draw in a wing. Now draw an arm and three claws (as shown).

4 Add a leg and foot with four claws. Draw in the shape of its crest.

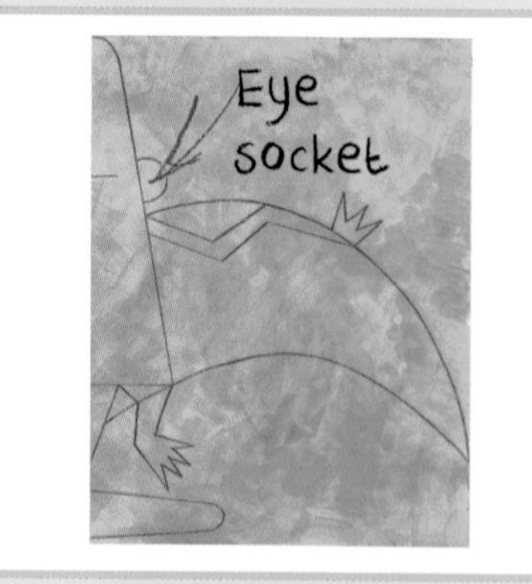

5 Draw in its eye socket.

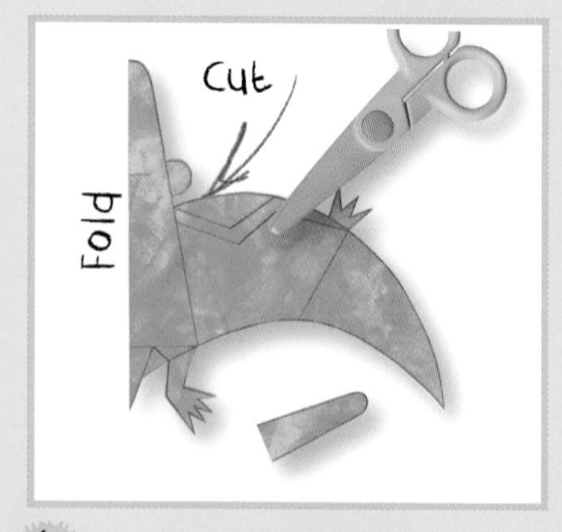

6 Cut out the Pteranodon. Then cut out its crest.

7 Open flat. Fold the wings upward along the black dotted lines. Fold the wing tips downward along the blue dotted lines (as shown).

Paint dark red stripes down its body. Add a pattern of long stripes to the wings.

Draw in the Pteranodon's eyes and nostrils, then paint its eyes.

Paint a dark red stripe down its crest shape. When dry, push the crest half-way into the slot in the Pteranodon's head (as shown).

Here are two more flying reptiles for you to try.

Torn Paper Stegosaurus

You will need:
- Pencil
- Sheet of thin white paper
- Sheet of coloured paper
- Coloured paper scraps
- Paper glue
- Poster paints
- Paintbrush

Make sure your hands are clean when you are tearing your paper.

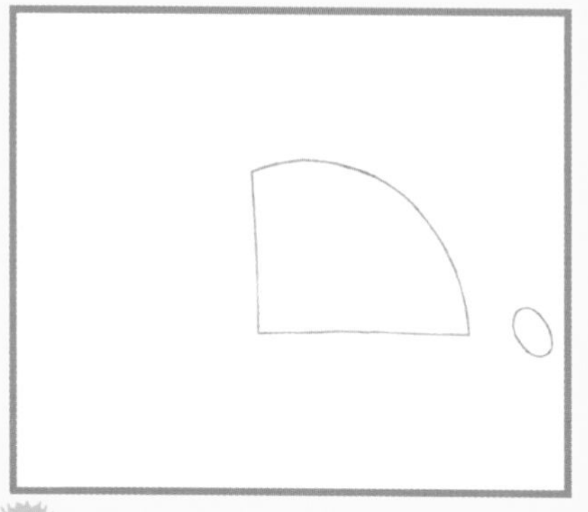

1 Pencil in simple shapes for the Stegosaurus's body and head.

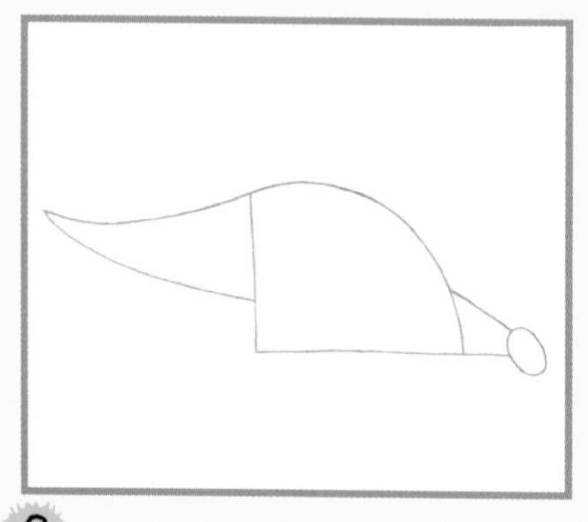

2 Now draw simple shapes for the neck and long tail.

3 Pencil in two small front legs and two thicker back legs.

4 Now draw pointed plates along the dinosaur's neck, back and tail. Draw big spots on its body and tail.

5 Scribble over the back of your drawing. Place on blue-coloured paper and press hard to transfer the drawing.

6 Use the transferred lines to tear out the shapes of the Stegosaurus's body, neck, head and tail.

7 Arrange the shapes onto coloured paper and glue in place.

Tear out shapes for some paper tree fern and cycad plants and glue them onto the background.

Paint in the Stegosaurus's eyes, nostrils and mouth. Draw in its toenails.

Collage Plesiosaurus

Use a variety of materials for your collage – the more the better!

You will need:
- Pencil
- Paper
- Scissors
- PVA glue
- Old sponge, magazine cuttings, corrugated paper, wrapping paper, buttons, foil, sequins

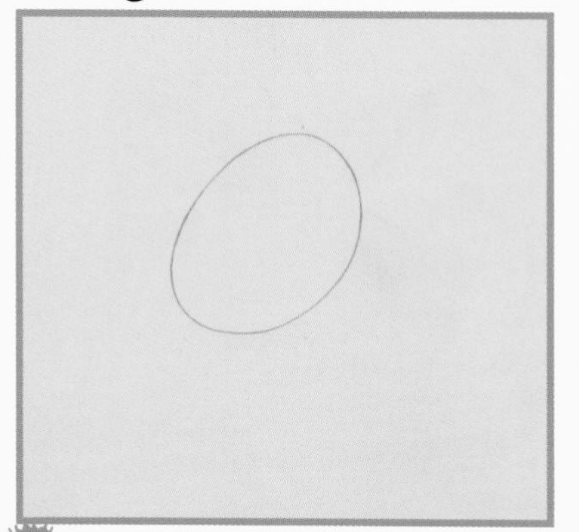

1 Pencil in an oval shape for the Plesiosaurus's body.

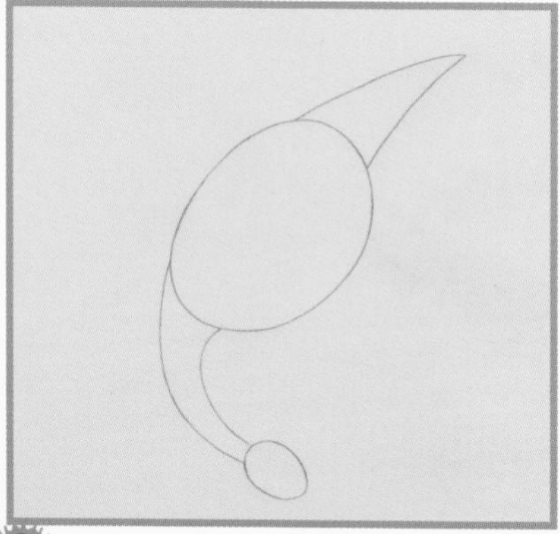

2 Draw in a long neck and tail. Add a small oval for the Plesiosaurus's head.

3 Pencil in four flippers. Scribble over the reverse side of your drawing.

4 Lay your drawing onto wrapping paper. Press the outline with a pencil to transfer the body shape. Cut out and glue onto the drawing.

5 Repeat step 4 for the neck and tail. Then use corrugated paper for the fins and head. Stick in place.

6 Glue on circles cut from magazines for the Plesiosaurus's markings. Use a button for its eye.

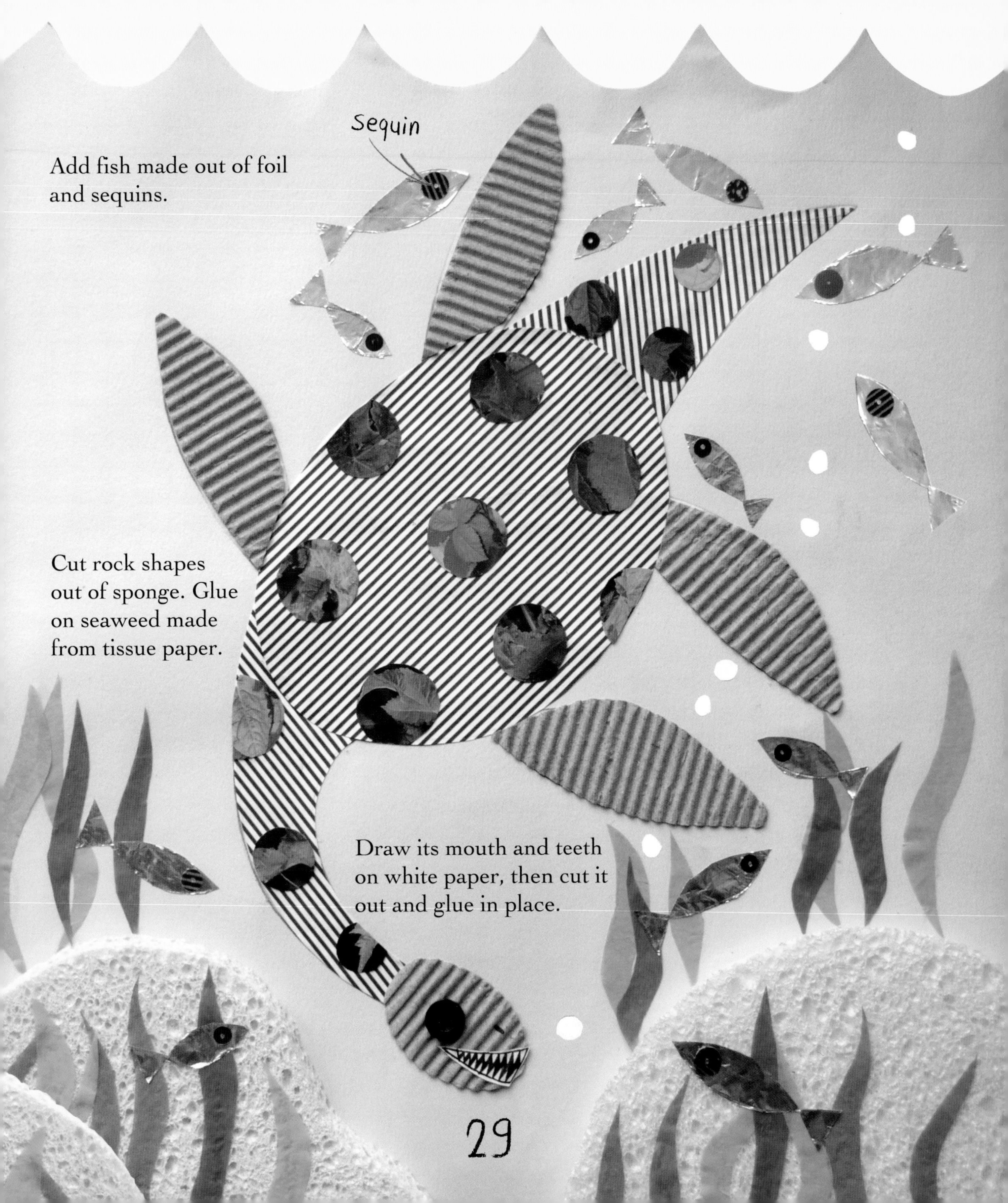

Add fish made out of foil and sequins.

Cut rock shapes out of sponge. Glue on seaweed made from tissue paper.

Draw its mouth and teeth on white paper, then cut it out and glue in place.

Mosaic Giganotosaurus

Make sure you ask an adult to help you cut your mosaic pieces.

You will need:
- Thick black paper
- Thin white paper
- Pencil
- White pencil crayon
- Coloured paper scraps
- PVA glue
- Plastic scissors

1 Pencil in the shape of the dinosaur's large head. Then draw in its body.

2 Now draw its neck and two small arms with three claws on each hand.

3 Pencil in the Giganotosaurus's eyes, nostrils, mouth and teeth.

4 Scribble over the back of your drawing with a white crayon. Turn over to transfer onto black paper.

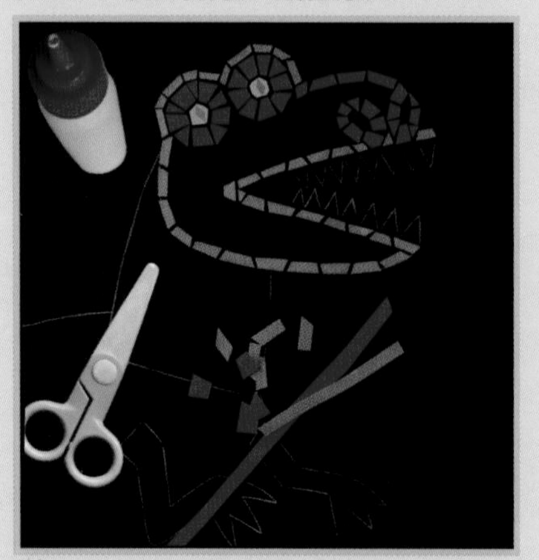

5 Cut strips out of coloured paper to cut into squares and triangles. Glue onto your drawing.

6 Use white triangles of paper for the teeth. Use green mosaics for the dinosaur's head and body.

7 Use orange, red and brown mosaics for the Giganotosaurus's neck and belly. Add green mosaics to the arms and white triangles for the claws.

Glossary

Collage an artwork made from various materials pasted onto a surface.

Cycad a type of plant that existed during the time of the dinosaurs.

Horsetail a type of prehistoric plant that covered entire forests in the time of the dinosaurs.

Mosaic an artwork made from small coloured pieces of glass or other materials.

Neck frill a curved bony plate extending behind the skull of certain dinosaurs.

Sail a sail-like structure on the back of various dinosaurs.

Tail club a bony mass at the end of the tail of some types of dinosaur.

Wax resist the use of a wax crayon to draw and block out areas from watercolour paint.

Index